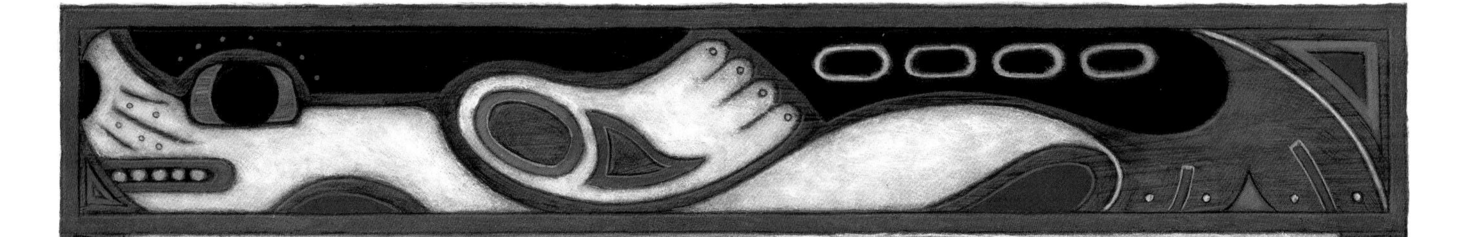

The Boy Who Lived With the Seals

Rafe Martin

Illustrated by David Shannon

G. P. Putnam's Sons • New York

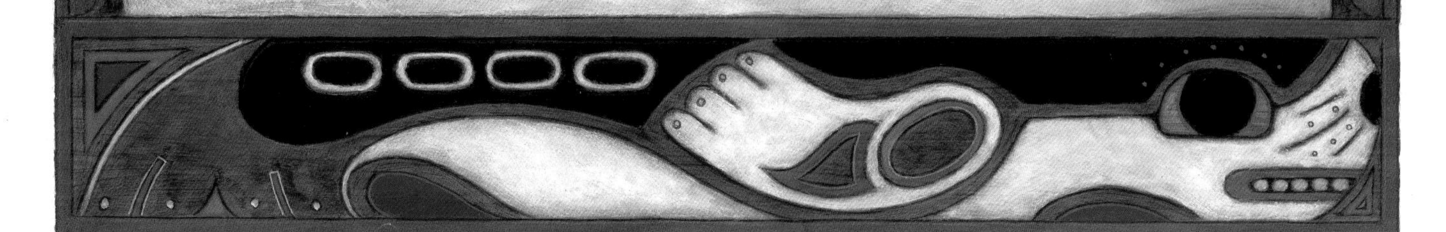

For Jacob and Ariya—hearing the call, finding their Ways.

—R.M.

To my wife, Heidi, and my godson Alec.

—D.S.

G. P. Putnam's Sons, a division of The Putnam & Grosset Group,
200 Madison Avenue, New York, NY 10016. Published simultaneously in Canada.
Printed in Hong Kong by South China Printing Co. (1988) Ltd.
Book design by Gunta Alexander. The text is set in Meridien.

Library of Congress Cataloging-in-Publication Data
Martin, Rafe, The boy who lived with the seals / by Rafe Martin ; illustrated by David Shannon. p. cm.
Summary: A lost boy who has grown up in the sea with seals returns to his tribe but is strangely changed.
1. Chinook Indians—Legends. [1. Chinook Indians—Legends. 2. Indians of North America—Legends.]
I. Shannon, David, ill. II. Title. E99.C57M37 1993 398.21'089974—dc20 [E] 91-46023 CIP AC
ISBN 0-399-22413-0
1 3 5 7 9 10 8 6 4 2
First Impression

Once the People were traveling on their spring migration and had camped along the shores of the great River.

One of the men was down by the River, working on his canoe. His little son, a boy of maybe five or six years, was there with him, playing in the water, tossing pebbles, and splashing by the shore.

As the man worked, the boy grew tired. After a time, he wandered off along the path that led back to the camp.

The sun began to sink, the shadows grew longer, and the man too headed back to his people. But when he reached the camp, he discovered that his son was not there. The parents called and called but there was no answer. The whole tribe began searching. They looked through the bushes by the River's edge, among the great trees of the forest, and along the foothills of the mountains. But there were no traces of the boy.

The elders said that the boy must have been carried off by a wild animal: wolf or bear or mountain lion. The others sadly loaded up their canoes and set off once more on their journey to the spring camp.

But the mother and father wouldn't leave. They stayed on for three more weeks, searching for their boy. It was dangerous for them to stay all alone like that in a place not their own. But after three weeks they too came to accept that their boy was indeed gone. So, with heavy hearts, they at last loaded up their canoe and paddled off, following their people.

Yet the parents never forgot the boy. They often remembered how he loved to play in the shallows of the River, how he could always be soothed by the sound of waves splashing.

One spring, when the People were again traveling, they met another tribe and they camped together. One night an old woman of the other tribe told an amazing story. "There is an island," she said, "near where the River empties into the sea. The seals love that island. When the sun is high, they haul themselves out on the rocks and lie there, drying their fur in the warm sun. And with those seals there is a boy."

When the mother and father heard this, their eyes opened wide. Their hearts began to beat with joy. And they were sure, *sure* it was their boy! Gathering some of the young men, they set off in their canoes until they came to that island. They hid themselves in the bushes along the shore and watched.

Sure enough, as the sun went up higher, the seals appeared. Their heads dotted the water as they rode the swells off the rocky shore. Then they clambered onto the rocks, shook the water from their wet fur, and lay contentedly basking and barking in the warm sun.

Last to come up out of the water was a boy—their boy!

Some of the young men slipped into the water and swam quietly out to the island. As they took hold of the boy, he began to cry out. Covering his mouth, they brought him back across the River to his parents and to his people.

But he was strange. He wouldn't talk, but only grunted and barked like a seal. He wouldn't walk, but only crawled on the ground. And he wouldn't eat the food that people eat. He only wanted raw fish, seaweed, and clams, like a seal.

Patiently his father taught him to walk again. His mother cooked the foods he had once loved and showed him again how to eat as a human being. Together his parents once more taught him the words and stories of his people. In time, the boy was almost as he had been before.

But not everything was quite the same. Child though he was, the boy now began to make canoes and paddles for his people. Each was carved and painted with designs of the sea and the sea's creatures. His people had never seen such beautiful things.

He began to make bows and arrows too. His bows were the strongest and his arrows flew farthest and straightest. But he never made them in the village. Always he would take his knives, branches, and tools down to the River where he would work alone.

Many nights the boy's father would have to come to get him from a perch where he sat overlooking the water. Sometimes it seemed to the father that he heard splashes in the darkness. And several times, when the moon was bright, he thought he saw sleek round heads disappearing into the water.

One night, when the People had built their fires, a faraway look came into the boy's eyes. Then he told them of his life under the sea with the seals. He said that the seals travel beneath the sea like the People travel on land.

He said that they build fires at night under the sea and tell stories. Only the stories the seals tell, he said, are of the things that happened long ago when the world was new, and of the things that are yet to happen far in the future.

His people listened. They felt the wonder of his tales, but they also felt the deep sea moving in his words and it made them uneasy. So they sat apart, staying distant from him. Only his parents dared come close. They touched his face and called his name to remind him of where he now was.

They tried to comfort him. "You have been gone a long time," they said, "but you will see. This is your place. These are your people."

But whenever his parents paddled across the River or out into the sea, the boy would hear the seals calling and would want to jump into the water and swim away with them. So his parents tied a deer hide over the boy, hoping he wouldn't see the seals, hoping he wouldn't hear them. And to distract him, they placed bowls of his favorite foods, pieces of fine-grained wood, and carving tools beside him under the hide.

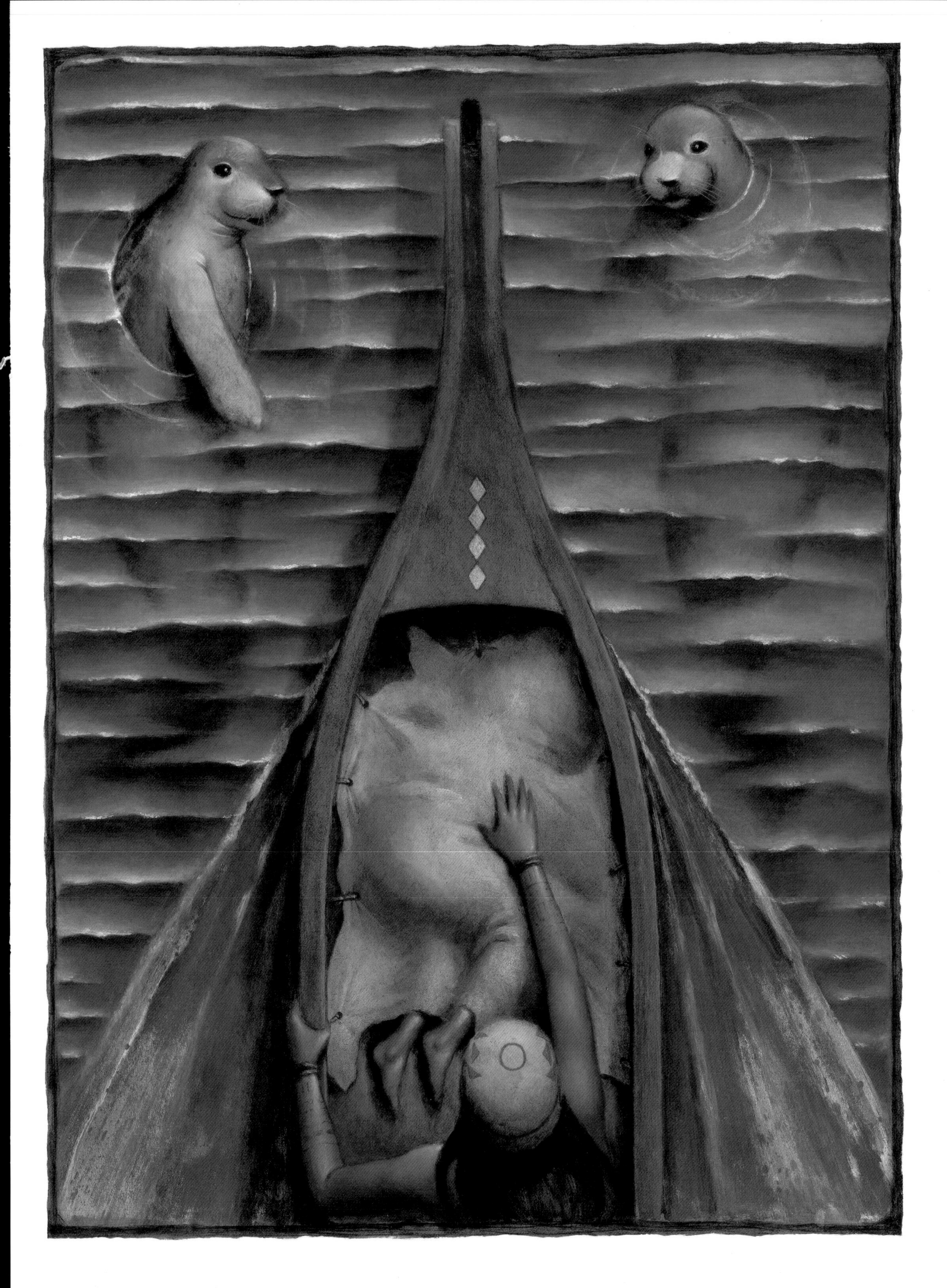

One day they were paddling across the great River, near where it emptied into the sea. Once again seals appeared and began calling. And the boy began struggling, struggling to be free. His parents paddled faster and faster. But it was no use. With a cry the boy tore a corner of the deer hide free, stood up, and dove over the side, down into the water.

Far out where the River emptied into the sea he reappeared again. Waving his hands over his head he called out, "Farewell, my parents, and do not grieve. I have another home under the sea and I'm going there!" Then he dove down down down down under the green sea.

His parents quickly paddled to the spot but it was too late. He was already gone. They placed his carving tools in a box and let it sink under the water. "Farewell," they said. "Remember us. We shall never forget you."

The following year, when his parents and people traveled to the spring camp, a beautifully carved canoe and paddle were waiting on the shore. In the canoe was the box in which the parents had placed the boy's carving tools.

After that, each spring, a new canoe and paddle were always waiting. And each year they were more beautifully made, more wonderfully painted and carved. And it eased the pain of missing him just a bit. For paddling those canoes, the parents and all the People could feel the joy of that boy who went to live with the seals.

AUTHOR'S NOTE

This story, *The Boy Who Lived With the Seals,* is based on a very short story told by the Chinook people of the Northwest Coast. For thousands of years they lived peacefully by the mouth of the Columbia River (the great River in our story) and along its inland shores fishing, rock-carving, trading, weaving beautiful baskets, and telling wonderful stories. They also traveled seasonally, visiting special places for hunting, camping, and root gathering.

Much more recently, when dams were built along the River, the People's villages, fishing sites, and rock carvings were all buried beneath the rising waters and they were forced to move farther inland. They are now part of the Confederated Warm Springs Tribes who live along the Deschutes River on the Warm Springs Reservation.

But like traditional peoples the world over, in their own language they call themselves simply, the People.

These People understand well the sacredness of all life. They know one cannot just take endlessly from nature's great reservoir of life, energy, and spirit without giving some gift in return—and that out of this gift new gifts of renewed life will grow.

The story, *The Boy Who Lived With the Seals,* is itself a gift from these generous People. But special thanks are also due to Jarold Ramsey, author of *Coyote Was Going There*, for his generosity and support in both permitting and encouraging me to tell this story in my way, for children today. It was from his fine book that the story itself and much of this information about it first came to me. Thanks also to Arthur Levine, my editor at Putnam's. After he heard me tell this traditional story he insisted I find a way to write it as a children's book.